Fourth of July

by Janet McDonnell
illustrated by Helen Endres

created by Wing Park Publishers

CHILDRENS PRESS®
CHICAGO

Library of Congress Cataloging-in-Publication Data

McDonnell, Janet, 1962-
    The Fourth of July / by Janet McDonnell ; illustrated by Helen
Endres.
       p.   cm. — (Circle the year with holidays)
    Summary: Nina and her poodle Sammy experience the sights
and sounds of a Fourth of July celebration. Includes crafts and tips
on fireworks safety.
    ISBN 0-516-00694-0
    [1. Fourth of July — Fiction. 2. Dogs — Fiction.] I. Endres,
Helen, ill. II. Title. III. Series.
PZ7.M47836Fm 1994
[E]—dc20
                                            94-4827
                                            CIP
                                            AC

Fourth of July

Early on the Fourth of July, Nina jumped
out of bed. She rushed to her dresser and pulled
out her blue shorts and the red and blue shirt
with stars.

"There," she said. "Red, white, and blue, just
like the flag." Then she said, "Come on, Sammy.
This is the best day of summer. I don't want
to miss anything."

After breakfast, Nina helped her dad decorate for the picnic. They put streamers, balloons, and flags all over the backyard. Nina even decorated Sammy. He didn't seem to mind.

Soon it was time for the picnic. Dad put
the hot dogs on the grill just as Nina's friend,
Susie, came from next door.

After lunch, Nina's mom came out with a cake with candles on it.

"Whose birthday is it?" asked Nina.

"It's our country's birthday," said her mother.

"But how can a country have a birthday?"

"Well, a long time ago, a king from England ruled the people who lived here. And he did not rule fairly," said her mom.

"The people wanted to be free from the king, so they created their own country, the United States of America. That was on July 4th in 1776."

"Well, let's sing Happy Birthday," said Nina. She started the song, and everyone joined in.

Suddenly, some big boys next door lit some firecrackers. BANG! Sammy did not like that one bit. He began barking and ran under the picnic table. "I don't think Sammy likes the Fourth of July," said Nina.

"It's OK, Sammy," said Nina. But Sammy would not come out. Not even for a hot dog. So Nina crawled under the table to pet him and make him feel better. "I don't like firecrackers either," she said. "But the Fourth of July is fun!"

Nina's dad looked at his watch. "The parade starts in ten minutes," he said. "We better hurry."

"Oh good, the parade!" said Nina. She and Susie ran to the gate. But then she looked back at Sammy. He looked so sad.

"Sammy wants to come too," said Nina. "Can I bring him?"

"Well, OK," said her dad. "But keep him on the leash."

"Now you'll see how much fun the Fourth can be," said Nina. She clipped Sammy's leash to his collar and wrapped the other end tightly around her hand. "Let's go," she said.

In the distance, Nina could hear the exciting sound of horns and drums from a marching band. "It's started! Let's hurry!" she said. When she turned the corner, Nina saw lots of people lined up to watch the parade.

   She and Susie squeezed their way to the front just in time to see a giant Uncle Sam on stilts. Behind him were some clowns. They were joking around and handing out balloons. Nina waved, hoping they would give her one.

Behind the clowns, Mayor Wilson and his wife were riding in the back of a slow-moving car. Mrs. Wilson was holding her cat Muffin and waving. Sammy hated that cat. Muffin jumped out of Mrs. Wilson's arms with a "MEOW!" Sammy took off after her, barking like crazy.

Sammy's leash was wrapped so tightly around Nina's hand that he pulled her along with him! "Stop, Sammy!" she yelled. But Sammy charged on.

He ran after Muffin, right through Mrs. Miller's flowers. He ran right through the sprinkler on the lawn next door. The red and blue streamers in his collar got wet, and the colors began to run.

"No, Sammy, stop!" shouted Nina.
"Somebody catch Muffin!" cried Mrs.
Wilson.
But Sammy charged on.

A man on the sidewalk was waving a big flag. Nina ran right into it, pulling the flag out of his hands. "Sorry!" she yelled over her shoulder.

Muffin ran right in front of the marching band, with Sammy close behind her.

Just then, all the drummers began playing
together, making a huge "BAM! baBAM!
baBAM!" It scared Sammy so that he forgot
all about Muffin. With a yelp, he took off down
Main Street.

The people along the parade route all laughed and pointed at Nina and Sammy. They made quite a sight.

As they ran past the speakers' stand, Nina heard the man with the microphone say, "My, my! A red, white, and blue dog. What a patriotic poodle!"

"Sammy! Stop this minute!" yelled Nina.

At last the drummers stopped drumming, and Sammy stopped running. They were at the end of the parade route. "You bad dog," said Nina after she caught her breath. Just then her parents came running.

"Are you all right?" asked her mom.

"Yes, but I'm never taking Sammy to a parade again," said Nina.

Then she said, "Did Mrs. Wilson find her cat?"

"Yes, Muffin is safe and sound," said her dad. "But we need to take this flag back to that poor man you almost ran over."

Nina laughed. "And after that, I think Sammy could use a bath."

As Nina, her parents, and Susie made their way home, they saw a crowd by the speaker's stand. "What's going on?" asked Nina.

"I don't know," said her dad. "Let's go see."

The man with the microphone was pinning a blue ribbon on a boy with a decorated bicycle. Everyone clapped.

Then the man with the microphone said, "And first prize for the 5 to 8 age group goes to . . . the patriotic poodle and his flag-waving owner!"

"Hey! That's you!" cried Susie. Everyone around clapped and cheered.

"Go on," said her mom, pushing her toward the stage. As the man tied a big blue ribbon to Sammy's collar, Nina decided she would wait until tomorrow to give her dog a bath.

That night, Nina and Susie watched the
fireworks from the front lawn. Nina's parents
sat on the front steps. Nina kept her arm around
Sammy so he wouldn't be afraid. People
walking by stopped to admire the red, white
and blue dog. Sammy held his head high, as
if to show off his blue ribbon.

As the sky burst into beautiful colors, Nina could hear her neighbors say "Ooh" and "Aaaah." Nina gave Sammy a big hug. "See?" she said. "I told you the Fourth of July was fun." Sammy barked in agreement.

ACTIVITY PAGES

Fireworks Safety

Fireworks are a fun part of the Fourth of July, but they can also be very dangerous! Every year, people get hurt setting off fireworks. In many places, fireworks are against the law. To have a safe and happy Fourth of July, remember to follow these rules:

1. If you find a firecracker, bottle rocket, or any kind of fireworks, don't touch it—even if you think it has already been used. Tell an adult about what you found.

2. If you see someone lighting fireworks, stay a safe distance away.

Many towns have a special fireworks show for everyone to enjoy. That's the safest way to have fun with fireworks on the Fourth!

Feather Pen Fun

The Fourth of July is the United States' birthday! On that day over two hundred years ago, the leaders of our country signed a paper called the Declaration of Independence. It said that the United States was now free from the king of England.

When those leaders signed the Declaration of Independence, they did not use the kind of pen we use today. They used a quill pen, made from a feather. You can make a feather pen. Here's how:

You will need:

—a large feather (the kind sold in craft stores work well)

—scissors

—tempera paint

—paper

1. Cut the pointy stem of the feather at an angle, as shown. This part is called the quill. (It may already be cut at an angle if the feather was bought at a craft store.)

2. Dip the point into a cup of paint. (You may need to thin the paint with a little water.) Pretend the paint is your ink. Now practice writing with your pen. Can you make thick and thin lines? Pretend you are signing the Declaration of Independence!

Fireworks Art!

Here are two ways to make fireworks pictures:

1. Blow Painting

Put some red tempera paint in one cup and some blue in another. Add a little water to thin the paint. With an eye dropper or a spoon, make a small puddle of paint on a piece of white paper. Use a straw to blow the paint out in different directions. (Do not touch the paint with the straw.)

2. "Magic" Painting

On a heavy piece of white paper, use lots of colored crayons to draw fireworks. You may want to make starburst patterns, as shown. Press hard with the crayons. When you are done, paint over the paper with thin black paint. The crayon will show through the paint to look like fireworks in a night sky!